THE SUPER SPEEDY SHARK

Look out for this little crab
as you read the story.

Sammy the shark can't help chomping things as she rushes around. She always seems to be late!

Sammy is on her way to school. She races for the school bus, but accidentally takes a bite out of it. CHOMP!

At school they all line up ready to go in but Sammy is last off the school bus and rushes to the line. Oh dear, she's knocked into everyone! At least she hasn't chomped anyone this time.

Sammy's so late for class that she rushes to her classroom, speeding into the teacher's desk. GOBBLE!

Lunchtime! Sammy can't wait to sit with her friends, but in her excitement she takes a chunk out of the lunch table. CRUNCH!

MUNCH!

During Maths, when Sammy knows the answer, she zooms up to the board, but can't stop! NIBBLE!

Time for sport and Sammy can't wait to catch the ball, but oh no, it's happened again. GULP!

MUNCH!

Sammy, how would you like to enter a swimming race?

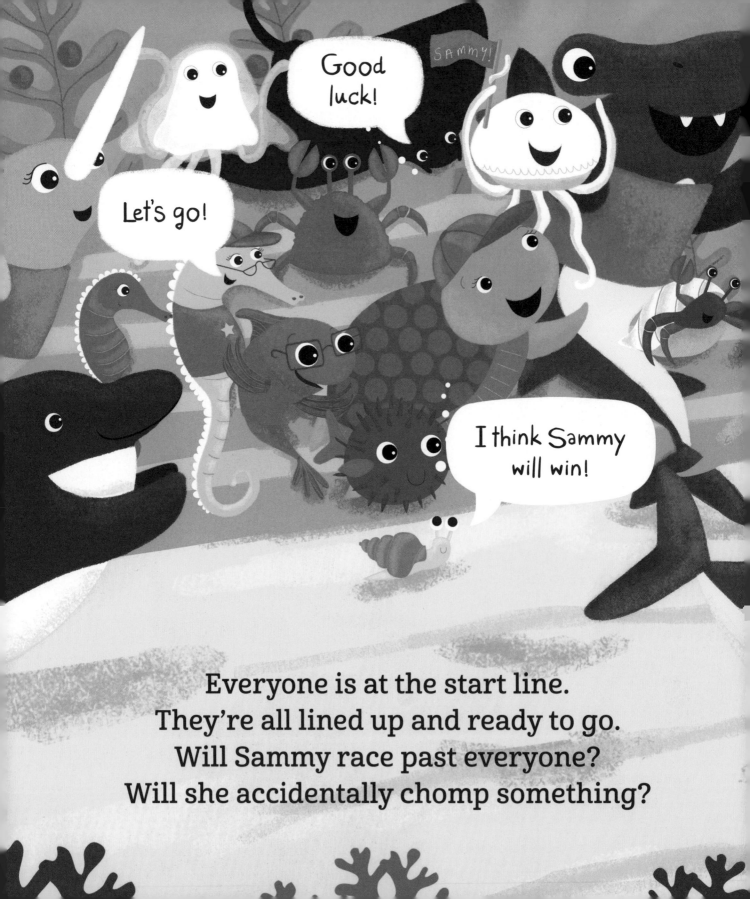

Everyone is at the start line.
They're all lined up and ready to go.
Will Sammy race past everyone?
Will she accidentally chomp something?

Sammy swims so fast she beats everyone else.
She shoots towards the finish and guess
what . . . she doesn't eat the winner's cup!

Sammy is officially the fastest fish in the sea!
She has found something that she's really
good at. Hooray!

Her teachers are very proud of her and Sammy is delighted. Finally, being fast is a good thing!

Maybe she won't munch things by accident anymore.

The Super Speedy Shark

A LAUGHING LOBSTER BOOK 978-1-910764-63-3

Published in Great Britain by Laughing Lobster, an imprint of Centum Publishing Ltd.
This edition published 2022.

13 5 7 9 10 8 6 4 2

Illustrations by Sophie Hanton.

Laughing Lobster, an imprint of Centum Publishing Ltd, 20 Devon Square, Newton Abbot, Devon, TQ12 2HR, UK. Centum Publishing Ltd, 9/10 Fenian St, Dublin 2, D02 RX24, Ireland

books@centumpublishingltd.co.uk

LAUGHING LOBSTER, CENTUM PUBLISHING LIMITED Reg. No. 08497203

A CIP catalogue record for this book is available from the British Library.

Printed in China.